S0-DTD-248

Books inspired by the television series

Bibliothèque et Archives nationales du Québec and Library and Archives Canada cataloguing in publication

Jolin, Dominique, 1964-
[Drôles d'histoires. English]
Funny stories
(Toopy and Binoo from the television series)
Translation of: Drôles d'histoires.
Previously published as: Toopy's story; Toopy goes bananas; Sneezing Toopy; and, The big race. c2006.
For children.

ISBN 978-1-55389-051-5

I. Tremblay, Carole, 1959- . II. Simon, Karen. III. Title.
IV. Title: Drôles d'histoires. English.
PS8569.O399D7613 2007 jC843'.54 C2007-941338-2
PS9569.O399D7613 2007

These texts are adapted from the television series *Toopy and Binoo* produced by Spectra Animation Inc., with the participation of Treehouse. Original scripts by Brian Lasenby, Anne-Marie Perrotta, Tean Schultz and Steven Western. Writing director: Katherine Sandford

Collection director: Lucie Papineau
Artistic and graphic direction, and *Toopy and Binoo* typeface design by Primeau & Barey

Legal Deposit: 3rd Quarter 2007
Bibliothèque et Archives nationales du Québec
National Library of Canada

Dominique et compagnie
300 Arran Street, Saint-Lambert, Quebec, Canada J4R 1K5
Tel: 514 875-0327 Fax: 450 672-5448
E-mail: dominiqueetcie@editionsheritage.com

www.dominiqueetcompagnie.com

Printed in China

We acknowledge the support of the Canada Council for the Arts for our publishing program.

We acknowledge the financial support of the Government of Canada through the Book Publishing Industry Development Program (BPIDP) for our publishing activities.

Government of Québec – Publishing Program and Tax Credit Program – Gestion SODEC.

Toopy's Story

Text by Dominique Jolin and Carole Tremblay
English Text by Karen Simon
From the original script by Anne-Marie Perrotta and Tean Schultz
Illustrations taken from the television series *Toopy and Binoo*

Click!

“Good night Binoo,” says Toopy.

Click!

Binoo turns the light back on and shows a picture book to Toopy. “Oh, I get it. You want a story, right?” Toopy asks. “Well, okay, but just one. I’m reallllly tired!!!”

Toopy begins to read,
"Once upon a time..."
He yawns.
"There were two brave knights, Sir Toopy and Sir Binoo..."
He yawns again.
"That searched all over the kingdom for a dragon.
Suddenly, the two knights found one and bravely followed
it into the Enchanted Forest. Uh-oh, sorry Binoo, but
I can't finish the story... the last page is missing."

“But don’t worry. I’ll make up an ending.”
Toopy yawns, then mumbles, “So the two brave
knights went home and went to bed.
The End.”

Binoo doesn’t like that ending.
And neither does the dragon.

So Toopy suggests,
"The two knights continued to follow the dragon. They had walked for two hours in the Enchanted Forest when all of a sudden...

… they found a big, comfy bed!
The two knights climbed in and
went to sleep.
The End!”

Toopy’s happy. He thinks he’s finished the story. But Binoo and Mr. Dragon have other ideas. “All right,” says Toopy, “I’ll continue. The knights followed the dragon in the forest for a long, long time when, all of a sudden, they saw a tower. A tower much too tall to climb.”

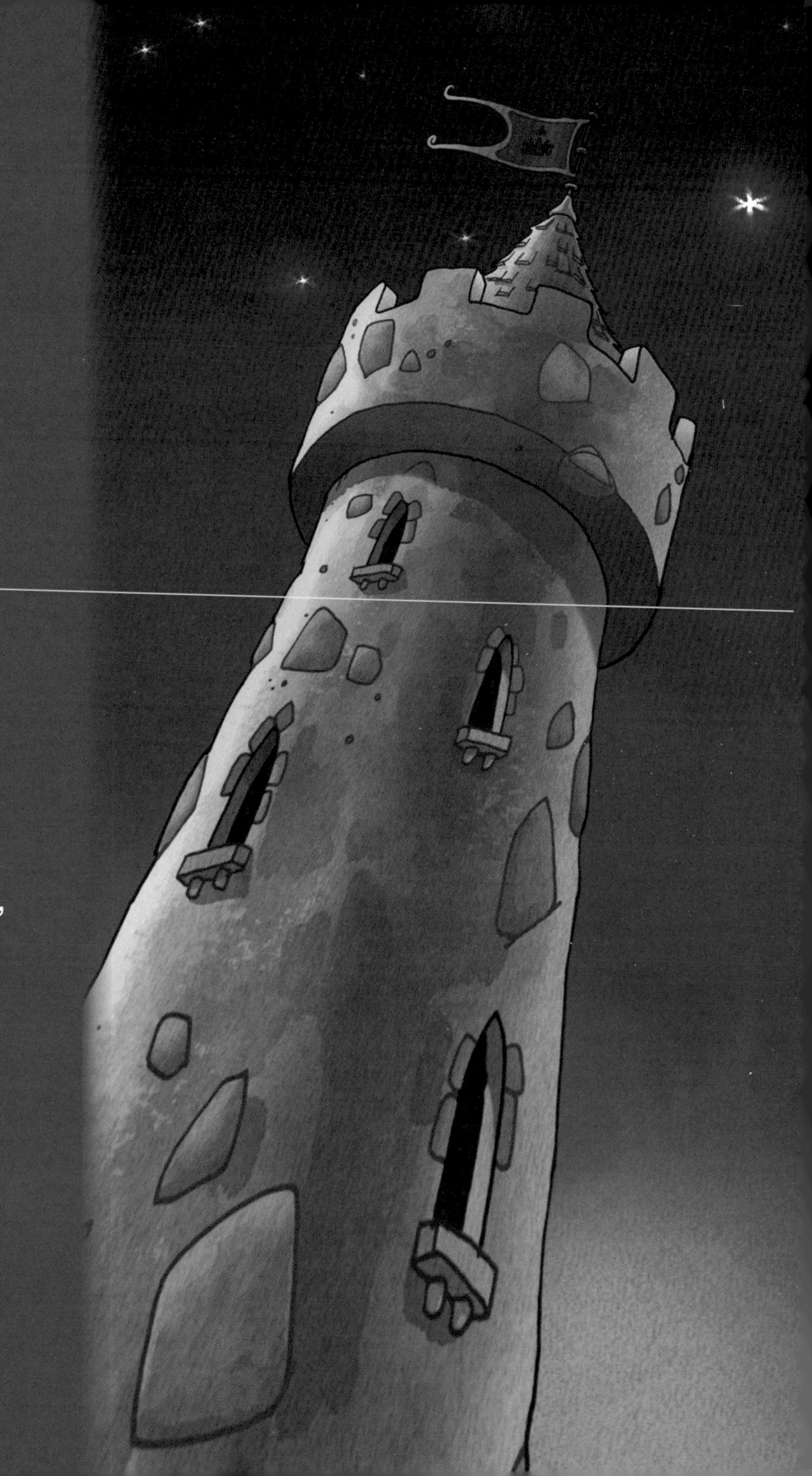

Before Toopy can finish his sentence, the dragon has already climbed the tower. Toopy doesn't want to follow him, but Binoo appears in a window. Toopy sighs.

“Oh fine, I’m coming.”

Toopy drags himself up the far, far too many stairs.
“Ohhh, it’s really high! And it’s really far!”

Toopy is exhausted when
he reaches the top. Still, he
continues the story,
“That’s when the two knights
found a fabulous, incredible,
amazing, big, comfy bed! Sir
Toopy climbed in right away
and fell asleep.
The End!”

Binoo shakes his head, “No.”
“No?” Toopy groans, quite
discouraged.

Toopy yawns an enormous yawn, and tries again.
“How about, the two knights found a dancing octopus?
A giant duck?… Not a giant duck.”

Toopy has no more ideas for finishing the story. But Binoo does, and he whispers something into Toopy's ear. Toopy thinks it's the best idea of all.

"At the top of the tower, the two knights found a really, really… beautiful lady dragon. It was love at first sight for Mr. Dragon. And for the lady dragon, too."

The dragon is happy. Binoo is happy. Toopy is happy. He's almost finished the story.

"And, as a reward for finding the end of
the story," Toopy adds, "The two brave knights
got the most extraordinary, comfy bed!
And the two dragons lived happily ever after.
The End."

Click!

“Nighty-night Binoo.”

Toopy Goes Bananas

Text by Dominique Jolin and Carole Tremblay
English Text by Karen Simon
From the original script by Steven Western
Illustrations taken from the television series *Toopy and Binoo*

“Hey! I hear a funny noise,” says Toopy.
“What is it? Oh! It’s your stomach growling Binoo!
That means it’s time for a snack.”

Toopy goes to get a bowl of fruit.
“What would you like Binoo? An apple or a banana?”
Binoo tries to take the banana, but... oops his book drops onto the floor.

“I’d really like a banana,” says Toopy.
Toopy takes the banana and begins to eat it while
Binoo picks up his book.

“What? You wanted a banana too? And I just ate the very last one...”
That’s okay. Binoo doesn’t mind eating the apple. But Toopy stops him.
“Wait! I know where I can get you another banana... I’ll be right back.”

Toopy goes to see Mr. Elephant.
“Hello, my name is Toopy. Binoo wanted a banana... but I ate
the last one. I was wondering if you could give me your banana?”
Mr. Elephant agrees. Toopy thanks him and leaves with
the banana.

"Here Binoo, I found a banana!" cries Toopy, coming into the house.
But Toopy slips on the banana peel he left on the floor earlier...
and falls right on the new banana that Mr. Elephant just gave him.
"Oops! I squished it. But don't worry, I think I know where I can
find another one."

Toopy takes a basket and flies into outer space.
"Hi there, my name is Toopy. Binoo would like a banana and
I was wondering if, by chance, you could give me one.
Yes? Oh, thank you very much!"

But while Toopy isn't looking the banana floats away into space.
When Toopy arrives home his basket is empty.
"You're going to laugh Binoo. I think I lost the banana this time.
But don't worry because I know another place where I can find
a delicious banana. Don't move. I'll be right back."

Toopy goes into the ocean.
"Hello, my name is Toopy. Binoo wanted a banana and..."
Before Toopy even finishes his sentence the fish gives him one!
"Oh, thank you! That's very generous of you."

This time Toopy's not taking any chances. He ties a piece of rope securely around the banana. "I always have such fabulous ideas," Toopy says, congratulating himself. "Thanks to me Binoo will finally be able to eat a delicious banana." But suddenly a whale comes along, finds the fruit appetizing and eats it.

Once again when Toopy arrives home the banana is gone.
"Um... keep on reading Binoo. I'll be right back."

Toopy has another idea. He pushes a big chest towards the high tower.
"I'm sure I've seen a banana around here..."

Toopy climbs to the top of the tower to see Mrs. Dragon.
"Good afternoon. My name is Toopy. Binoo wanted a banana, but someone lost it. So, I was wondering if..."
Mrs. Dragon kindly gives him her banana.
"For me? Thank you so very much!"

Toopy doesn't want to lose the banana this time. He plans very carefully how he can keep the banana safe.

Step one: Open the Banana Chest.
Step two: Put the banana inside.
Step three: Lock up the chest.

"Ta-dah! Now it's safe!"

Toopy has done it! He finally has a banana for his friend.
"I have a surprise for you Binoo. You'll never guess what it is.
But first, I have to open the Banana Chest. Hey!
Where's the key? It's got to be around here somewhere."
But Toopy can't find it anywhere.

At that very moment Binoo's stomach begins
to growl again.

"Your stomach is still growling!" Toopy offers the bowl of fruit to Binoo. "What would you like? An apple or some grapes?" Binoo tries to take the apple, but his book drops to the floor again.

"I really love apples," says Toopy. Toopy reaches for the apple, but Binoo is faster than Toopy and grabs the apple first.

This time Binoo will pick up his book after his snack!

Sneezing Toopy

Text by Dominique Jolin and Carole Tremblay
English Text by Karen Simon
From the original script by Anne-Marie Perrotta and Tean Schultz
Illustrations taken from the television series *Toopy and Binoo*

"Achoo!" Toopy sneezes so hard that Binoo's blocks come tumbling down.

"Sorry Binoo," says Toopy. "It's just that I'm feeling dizzy, my forehead is hot and when I bend my head over my nose runs."

Binoo leads Toopy to the sofa.
"What are you doing? Oh, you want me to rest.
That's so kind of you. Thanks Binoo!"

Toopy wipes his nose.
"Binoo? It's strange. Now my throat
is dry. I don't know what to do."
Toopy has the sniffles.

Binoo has an idea. “Water!” cries Toopy.
“That’s so kind of you. Thanks a lot.”

Binoo goes back to play with his blocks,
but Toopy calls him again.
“Binooo? You know what? I still feel dizzy and
my mouth is so far away from my glass.”

Binoo has just what Toopy needs: a straw.
“What a fabulous idea,” says Toopy. “Thanks again.”

"Aaa... Aaa... Achooo!"
Toopy sneezes once again. And once again
Binoo's blocks come tumbling down.
"Binooo? Are you there?" asks Toopy. "I'm sorry.
I thought everything was perfect, but... I'm actually
not very comfy. Have any ideas?"

Of course Binoo has an idea.

But none of the cushions are just right for Toopy.
They're either too hard, or too soft, or too big.

Binoo has another idea. He climbs to the top of
a mountain and brings back a cloud!

Toopy is de-light-ed.
"I think I might be feeling a little better," he says.

But…
"Aaa… Aaa… Achooo!" Binoo's blocks fall down again. "I don't know why, but I'm a bit cold now," says Toopy.

No problem. Binoo brings back the sun and holds it over the sofa. **"The sun!"** exclaims Toopy. "It's so nice and warm. It's perfect!" After hesitating a moment he adds, "But you know Binoo, the rays are too strong. They're hurting my eyes."

Binoo understands. He turns off the sun and “Click,”
the moon has taken its place.
“Aaah, that’s so much better. You’re wonderful Binoo.
I love you so much.”

Binoo doesn’t answer.
“Binooooo? Where are you?” asks Toopy.

Binoo comes back with a
funny-looking block. Toopy is intrigued.
“What’s that?” Toopy asks.

Binoo pulls on a string and “Poof,”
a piano appears.

Binoo puts on his gloves. Toopy is very excited.
"You're going to play for me? So I'll feel better? Oh, thank you, thank you Binoo!"

Binoo begins to play.
"That's so pretty!" Toopy sighs.

Toopy stretches and takes a deep breath. His nose isn't blocked anymore!
"You know what Binoo? I think I'm better. And it's all because of you. Now I can smile again, and sing, and dance, and talk and…"

“Aaa… Aaa… Achooo!”
Oh no! Now it’s Binoo that’s sneezing.
“Poor Binoo! Now you’re sick.
Wait, I’ll take care of you,” says Toopy.

Toopy settles his friend comfortably on the cloud.
“Now I’ll play *your* favourite song.”

"You'll soon feel much better. You'll see!"

The Big Race

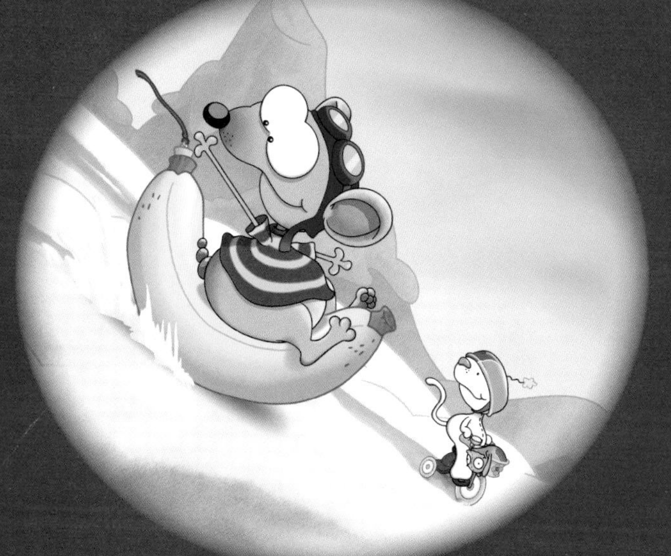

Text by Dominique Jolin and Carole Tremblay
English Text by Karen Simon
From the original script by Brian Lasenby
Illustrations taken from the television series *Toopy and Binoo*

“The biggest race ever is about to start!” Toopy exclaims. “THE GREAT BINOO, PATCHY PATCH and THE FABULOUS TOOPY are waiting at the starting line. Are you ready? All right. Get set, GO!!!”

At first Toopy is ahead, but Binoo pedals so hard that he soon takes the lead.

But what's happening? Oh no! Toopy has lost a wheel. Can he stay in the race?

Of course he can! Here he comes bouncing along.

Binoo is pedalling as fast as he can. He's ahead, but Toopy's even faster and jumps in front of him.

But now Toopy has a new problem. He's landed right in a gopher hole and he's stuck. Mr. Gopher doesn't look very happy.
Will Toopy be able to get back in the race?

Well, of course he can! Binoo wonders where Toopy is when all of a sudden he sees him. Here comes Toopy soaring into the lead.
Toopy's in his hot-air balloon!

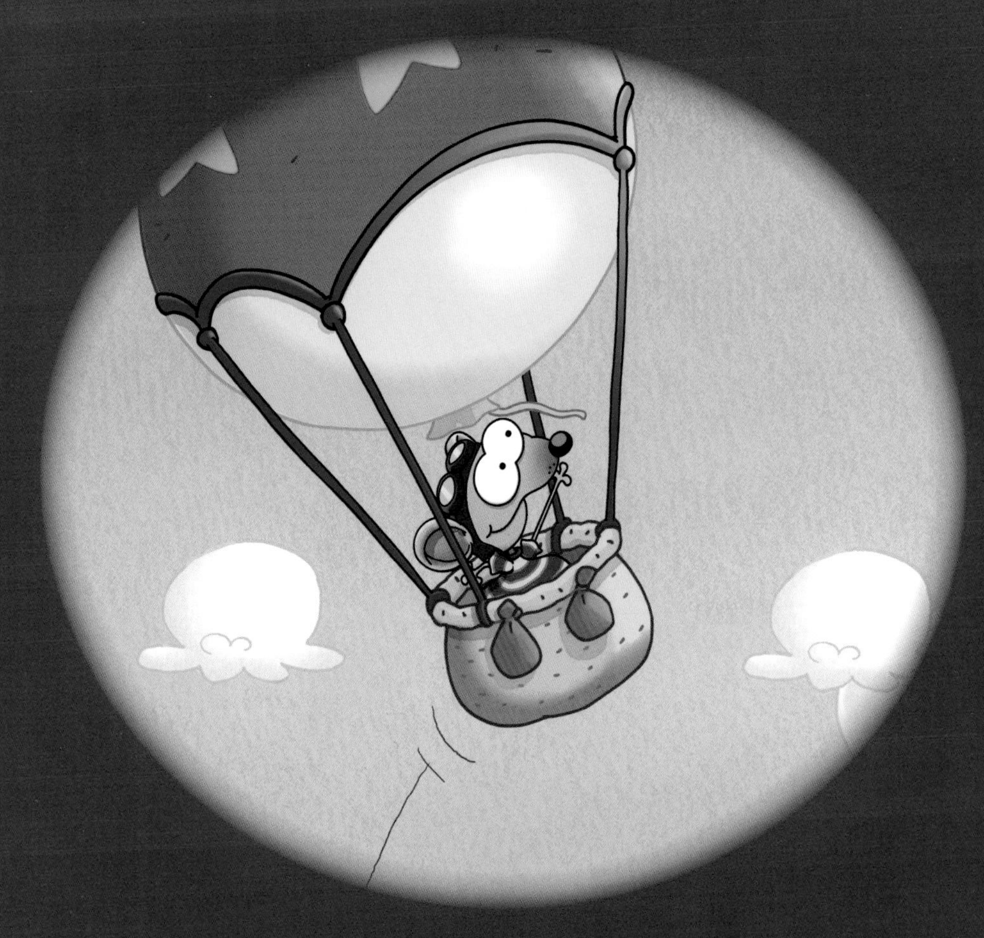

Oh look! Toopy sees a rope hanging from the balloon. "What's this doing here?" he wonders, pulling on the rope.

The balloon starts losing air. Whoops! Maybe Toopy should have left the rope alone. This little mistake lets Binoo move back into the lead. But not for long because…

The Fabulous Toopy is back faster than ever!
He's not even trying to win, but he's winning anyway!
But what's that funny thing hanging out of the
banana?

Oops! Toopy probably shouldn't have pulled
on the cord.

Binoo continues to pedal. He thinks he's in the lead and far ahead of Toopy.

But Toopy's back in the race. This time he isn't in the air, nooo, he's down in the water. Toopy, the most fabulous racer in the world, is zooming past Binoo on his incredible sea serpent.

Oh, there's a bobber floating on the water.
Toopy pulls and pulls… and pulls…

Oops! Maybe Toopy shouldn't have pulled on the bobber. It was attached to the plug and the river is draining. Is it all over for Toopy? Has he lost the race? And just before reaching the finish line?

Can Toopy, the most spectacular racer in the world, come in second? Of course NOT! Toopy and Binoo are now neck and neck. It looks like there will be a tie. Who will win the big race?

Oh no! Toopy and Binoo's race car hits a bump!

And it's Patchy Patch crossing
the finish line first. Bravo!
Patchy Patch is the greatest
racer in the world!